Why Not Call It Cow Juice?

by Steven Krasner

Illustrated by Sandy Griffis

Text copyright © 1994 by Steven Krasner
Illustrations copyright © 1994 by Sandy Griffis
All Rights Reserved. This edition published by Gorilla Productions
Second Gorilla Productions Printing, 1995
Third Gorilla Productions Printing, 1999
Fourth Gorilla Productions Printing, 2007

Gorilla Productions

Library of Congress Catalog Card Number 94-96228
ISBN 0-9642721-0-5

Amy and Jeffrey sat down at the kitchen table, ready to eat their lunch.

"What would you like to drink?" asked Dad.

"I want some milk, please," said Jeffrey.

"Some what?" asked Dad, opening the refrigerator door.

"Some milk," repeated Jeffrey.

"You mean cow juice?" asked Dad, holding up a big bottle of white liquid.

"That's not cow juice, it's milk," said Amy.

"Now wait a minute," said Dad. "What do you get from apples?"

"Apple juice," said Amy.

"And what do you get from oranges?" asked Dad.

"Orange juice," said Jeffrey.

"And what do you get from grapefruits?" asked Dad.

"Grapefruit juice," said Amy.

"So what do you get from cows?" asked Dad, with a wide, triumphant smile.

Amy and Jeffrey looked at each other.

"You get milk," said Amy, giggling.

"They don't call it cow juice," said Jeffrey.

"Why not?" asked Dad.

Before Amy and Jeffrey could respond to that question, Mom walked into the kitchen, carrying Emily.

"I have the baby ready to go," said Mom. "Let's go out for a while after you finish lunch. I have a few errands I'd like to do."

So Amy and Jeffrey finished their tuna fish sandwiches.

Then the family members hopped into the car, buckled up their seat belts and set off for a drive.

"The first stop is Bayberry Lane," said Mom. "I want to check out a garage sale."

Dad drove to Bayberry Lane and pulled over where Mom saw the sale.

"I thought this was a garage sale," said Dad as Mom looked through an assortment of old books, clothes and furniture. "I don't see any garages for sale. Why do they call it a garage sale?"

"I know why," said Amy. "My teacher told us. It's because all this stuff was in the garage and the people who live here don't want it anymore."

"That's right, dear," said Mom. "A garage sale is just an expression. There aren't any garages for sale."

"Why not?" asked Dad.

Mom didn't answer. She was done browsing, so they gathered up Amy, Jeffrey and Emily and got back in the car.

"Let's go to the department store down the street," said Mom. "There's something I want to check out."

Dad drove to the department store. He parked the car and everyone got out.

"They're having a white elephant sale here," said Mom.

"A what?" screamed Dad. "What do we want with a white elephant? How would we give it a bath? It wouldn't even fit in our bathtub!"

"It's just an expression," said Mom, pushing Emily in the stroller. "They call all strange, one-of-a-kind items 'white elephants.' There aren't any real white elephants for sale."

"Why not?" asked Dad.

Mom, shaking her head slightly, ignored Dad's question. She was done looking at white elephants. It was time to leave, so again, the family piled into the car.

"I have one more place I'd like to visit," said Mom. "It's just down the street. Take a right, please."

Dad did as Mom asked. He pulled into a busy parking lot.

"This is the flea market I wanted to see," said Mom.

"The what?" bellowed Dad. "We don't need any fleas. They make me itch."

"Dad," said Jeffrey, rolling his eyes. "They don't sell fleas here. I know. I saw one of these flea markets in a cartoon."

"Jeffrey's right," said Mom, looking at all the merchandise on display. "It's just another expression. A flea market has a lot of odds and ends. They don't sell any fleas."

"Why not?" asked Dad.

Mom just smiled patiently.

"I'm all done looking," she said.

"And I'm hungry for some dessert," said Dad. "I know a nice place where we can get some dessert."

So Dad drove to a nearby pastry shop. The family went in and sat down at a big round table.

They looked at the menu. A short time later, a waitress came to take their order.

"I'll have some chocolate mousse," said Dad. "But I don't want any antlers."

"Sir, chocolate mousse doesn't have any antlers," said the waitress quickly.

"Listen, I've seen plenty of those animals, and they all have antlers," insisted Dad.

"Dear," said Mom. "That's moose, M-O-O-S-E, not chocolate mousse, M-O-U-S-S-E. Moose have antlers. Chocolate mousse does not."

"Oh, well, anyway, that's what I'll have," grumbled Dad.

"And what would you like to drink?" asked the waitress.

"I'll have cow juice," said Dad.

"Cow juice?!" asked the waitress.

"Dad, they call it milk," said Jeffrey, exasperation in his voice. "They don't call it cow juice."

"Why not?" asked Dad.

Mom, Amy and Jeffrey exchanged knowing glances while Emily banged a spoon on the table.

"This has been an interesting day," said Mom, smiling at Amy and Jeffrey. "I have another one planned for next Saturday, too."
"What are we going to do?" asked Amy.

"We're going to a farmers' market," said Mom.

"You mean a market where they only sell farmers?" asked Dad. "We don't even live on a farm."

"You'll see," said Mom, chuckling sofly.

The next Saturday was a bright, sunny day. After finishing breakfast, Amy, Jeffrey, Emily, Dad and Mom got into their car. They buckled up their seat belts and set off for the farmers' market.

It took a while to drive to the farmers' market. And when they got to it, there were many farmers there.

But to Dad's confusion, not one farmer was for sale.

"Then why do they call it a farmers' market?" asked Dad.

"Because what farmers grow or raise on their farms is sold here," said Mom.

After putting Emily in the stroller, Mom pulled out her shopping list.

"Let's go look at the vegetables," she said. "I want to buy some ears of corn."

"Ears of corn? Do farmers grow ears of corn?" asked Dad.

"Of course they do," said Amy.

"Right on the sides of their heads?" asked Dad. "How do farmers hear anything with vegetables growing out of their heads? I've never heard of anything so silly."

"Dad, ears of corn grow on stalks out in the field," said Jeffrey. "They can't hear."

"Why not?" asked Dad.

Mom, not really listening to Dad, scooped up a dozen ears of corn.

"Now I want a head of lettuce," said Mom.

"A what?" shrieked Dad. "Do you mean to tell me there is a vegetable that has eyes, a nose, a mouth, ears and hair on top?"

"No, dear," said Mom gently, reaching for a nice, rounded head of lettuce. "It just kind of looks like a head, that's all."

"Well," said Dad. "You better get two of them. Two heads are better than one, you know."

"Thanks, dear," said Mom. "And now I see some artichoke hearts I'd like to have for tonight's salad."

"Artichoke hearts?" asked Dad. "Are they still beating?"

"No, they're not still beating," said Mom, beginning to lose her patience. "It's just the center part of the artichoke. They call it a heart, that's all."

Mom gathered up some artichoke hearts. Then she filled her basket with other fruits and vegetables.

Finally, Mom walked over to the meat department, followed by Amy, Jeffrey and Dad, who was pushing Emily's stroller.

Mom selected a roast.

"What's that?" asked Dad.

"It's an eye of the round," said Mom.

"An eye?" yelled Dad, his own eyes widening. "Who wants to eat something that can look back at you while you're cutting it up?"

"Dad, you're gross," groaned Amy.

"That's disgusting," moaned Jeffrey.

"It's merely a name for a particular cut of meat," said Mom wearily. "Let's go. I've done enough shopping for one day."

"I know a place where we can stop for a snack," said Dad brightly as the family headed back to the car.

He drove for a short time and pulled into the parking lot for a sandwich shop.

The family walked in and sat down at a table. A waiter approached the table as the family studied the menu.

"Would you like our special bottomless cup of coffee?" the waiter asked Dad.

"A bottomless cup of coffee?" spouted Dad. "What a mess that will make. Really! A cup with no bottom. All the coffee will spill on the floor. We'll have to put on our bathing suits because we'll be swimming in coffee if you keep pouring it into a bottomless cup."

"Dear," said Mom firmly. "He doesn't mean a cup without a bottom. It's just an expression that means he'll refill your cup whenever it's empty."

"Oh," said Dad. "Well, never mind. Just bring me a glass of cow juice, please."

"Cow juice, sir?" asked the astonished waiter.

"Dad," cried Amy and Jeffrey in an exasperated chorus. "They call it milk. Thay don't call it cow juice."

"Why not?" asked Dad.

The family finished its snack and drove home.

When they walked in, Dad noticed a pile of laundry that had to be put away.

"Give me a hand with this laundry, please," said Dad to Amy and Jeffrey.

Amy and Jeffrey looked at each other and smiled. They began clapping their hands, applauding their Dad.

"Yeah, way to go, Dad," laughed Amy.

"All right, Dad," smiled Jeffrey.

"That's not what I meant and you know it," said Dad. "Now don't make me yell because I'm losing my voice."

"We'll help you find it," said Amy, giggling.

"I think I saw it in the kitchen," offered Jeffrey, grinning at Amy.

"Now listen here," began Dad, becoming annoyed.

But just then, Mom walked by, holding Emily. She winked at Amy and Jeffrey.

"Dear, why don't you come into the kitchen and have a glass of cow juice?" she asked Dad.

Dad looked at Mom. And he looked at Amy, Jeffrey and Emily. And he smiled.

"Why not?"